THIS WALKER  BOOK BELONGS TO:

_____

_____

_____

DISCARDED

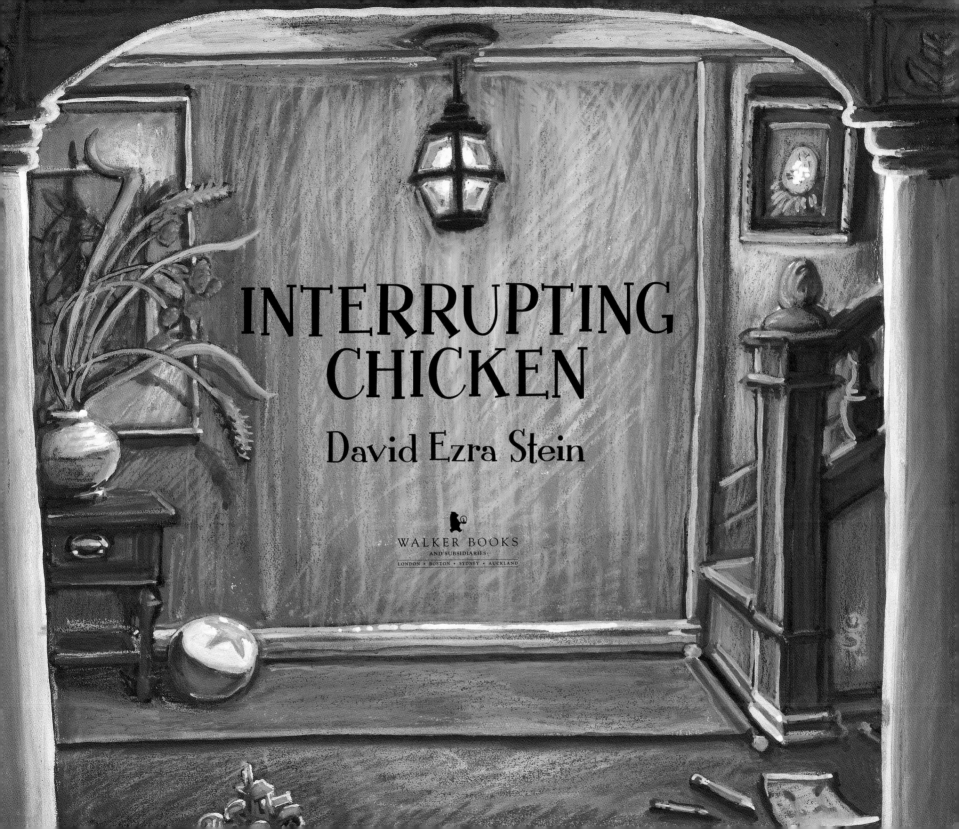

INTERRUPTING CHICKEN

David Ezra Stein

WALKER BOOKS
AND SUBSIDIARIES
LONDON · BOSTON · SYDNEY · AUCKLAND

It was bedtime for the little red chicken.

"OK, my little chicken," said Papa.
"Are you all ready to go to sleep?"

"Yes, Papa! But you forgot something."

"What's that?" asked Papa.

"A bedtime story!"

"All right," said Papa. "I'll read one of your favourites.
And of course you are not going to *interrupt*
the story tonight, are you?"

"Oh no, Papa. I'll be good."

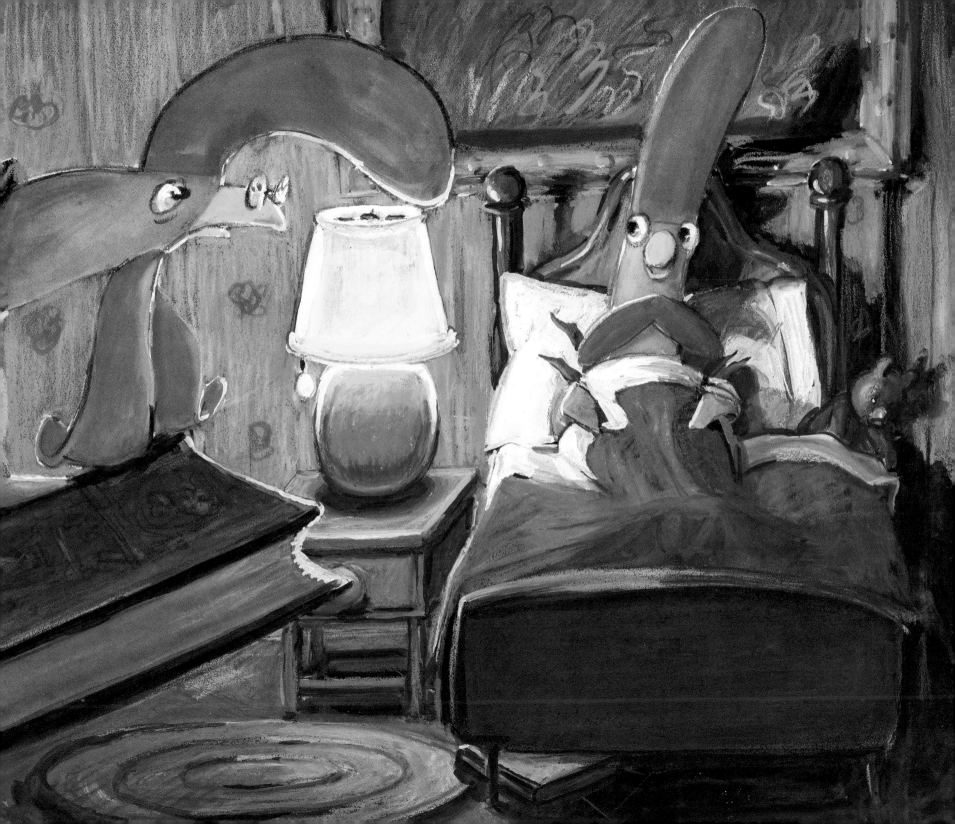

Hansel and Gretel were very hungry. Deep in the woods they found a house made of candy. Nibble, nibble, nibble; they began to eat the house, until the old woman who lived there came out and said, "What lovely children! Why don't you come inside?" They were just about to follow her when—

"Chicken."

"Yes, Papa?"

"You interrupted the story. Try not to get so involved."

"I'm sorry, Papa. But she really was a witch."

"Well, you're supposed to be relaxing so you can fall asleep."

"Let's try another story. I'll be good!"

"Take this basket of goodies to Grandma," said Little Red Riding Hood's mother. "But don't stray from the path. The woods are full of danger." Little Red Riding Hood skipped along through the deep woods. By and by she met a wolf who wished her "Good morning." She was about to answer him when—

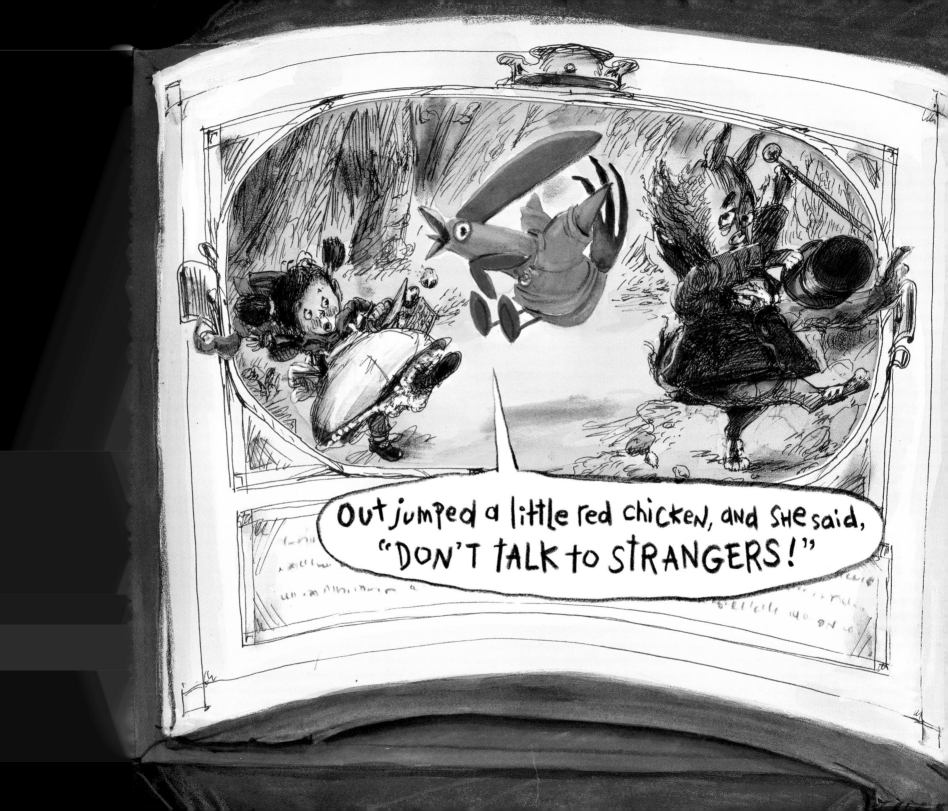

"Chicken."

"Yes, Papa?"

"You did it again. You interrupted two stories, and you're not even sleepy!"

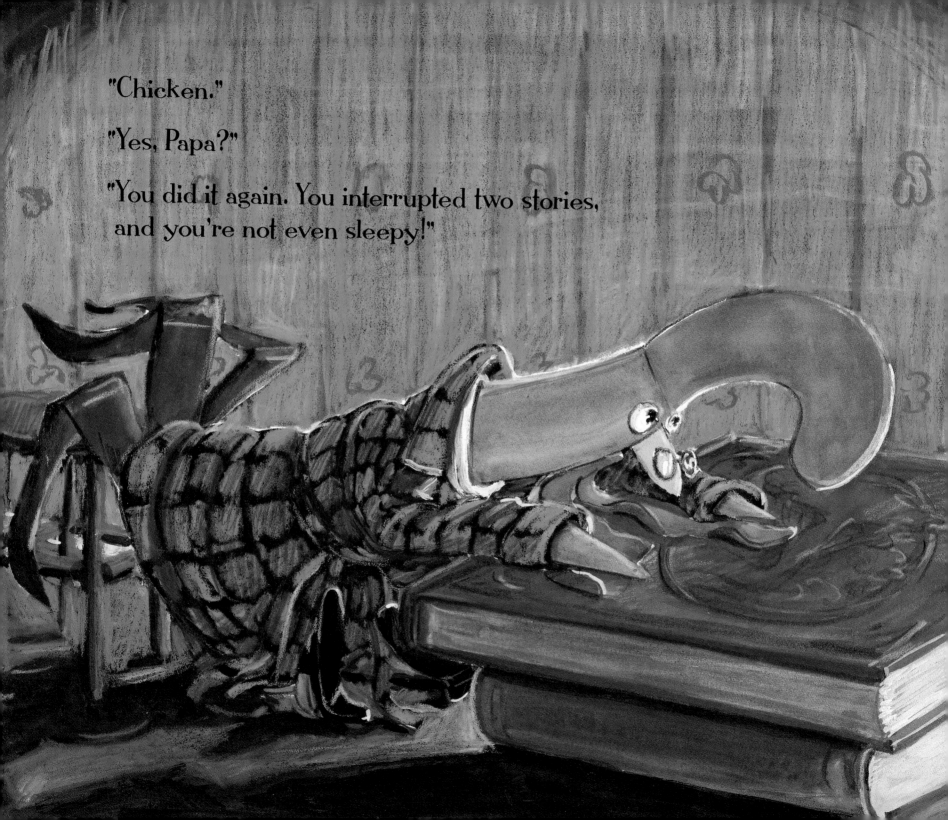

"I know, Papa! I'm sorry. But he was a *mean* old wolf."

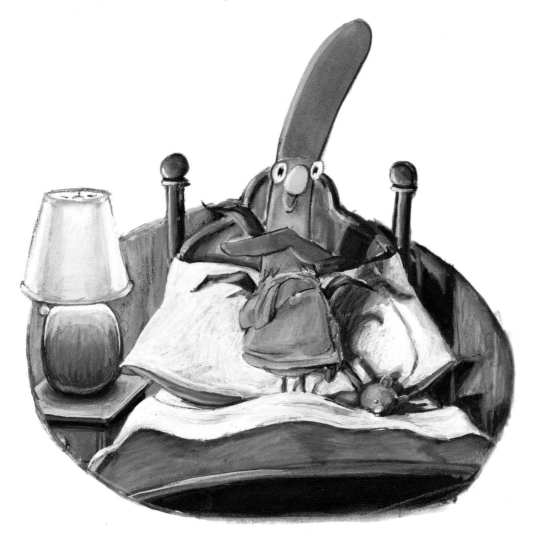

"Yes. Now get back into bed."

"OK, Papa. Let's try one more *little* story, and I'll be good!"

Chicken Little was hit on the head by an acorn. *The sky is falling!* she thought.
She was about to run off and warn Goosey Loosey, Ducky Lucky, Henny Penny
and everyone on the farm that the sky was falling when—

"Oh, Papa. I couldn't let that little chicken get all upset over an acorn! Please read *one more* story, and I promise I'll fall asleep."

"But Chicken," said Papa, "we've run out of stories."

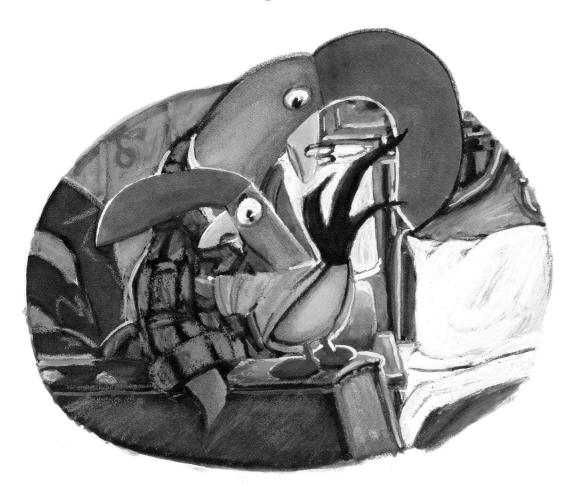

"Oh no, Papa. I can't go to sleep without a story!"

"Then," said Papa, yawning, "why don't *you* tell *me* a story?"

"*Me* tell a story?" said the little red chicken. "OK, Papa! Here we go! Um..."

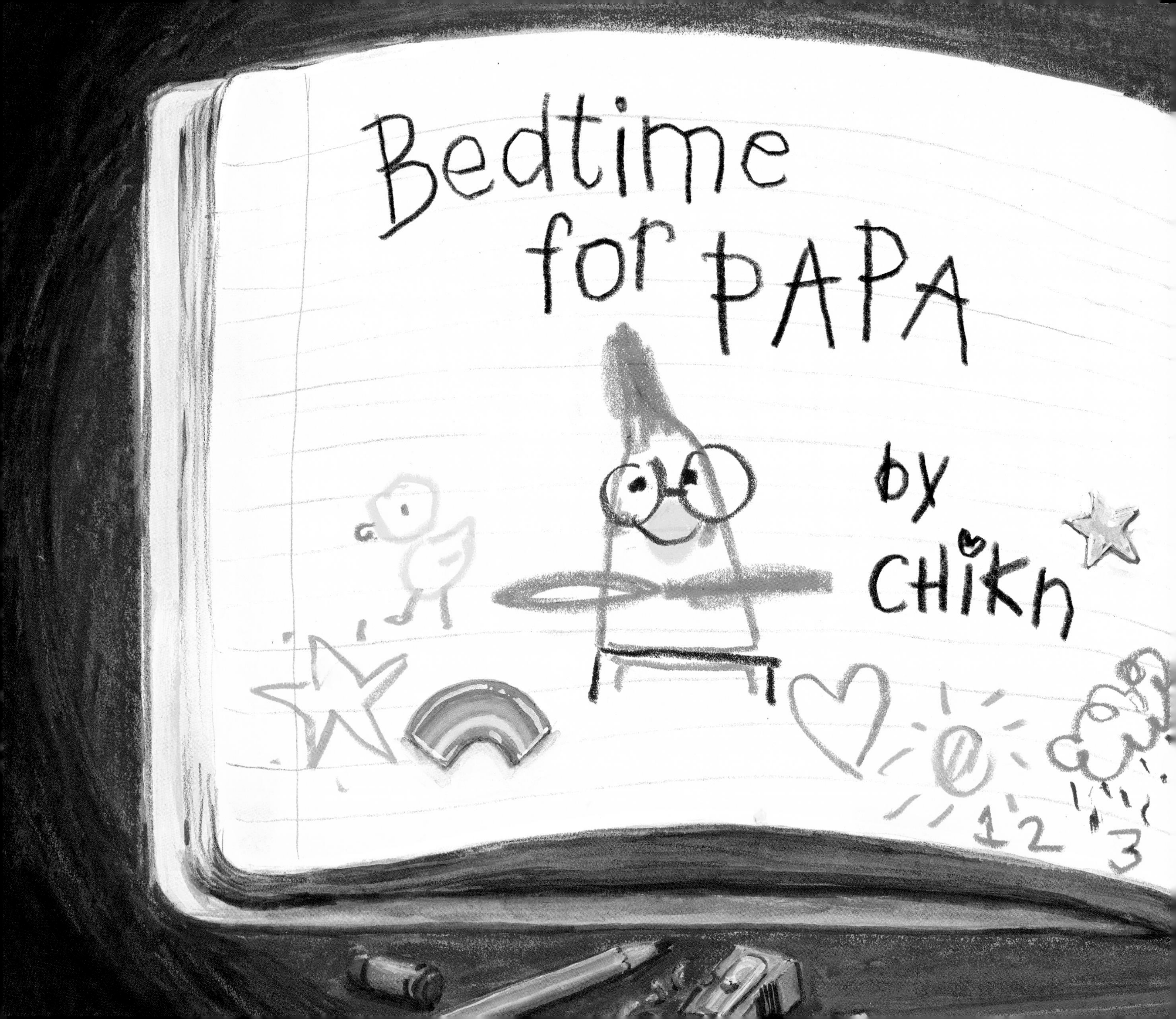
Bedtime
for PAPA
by
CHikn
1 2 3

Once there was a little red chicken who put her Papa to bed. She read him a hundred stories. She even gave him warm milk, but nothing worked: he stayed wide awake all—

"Goodnight, Papa."

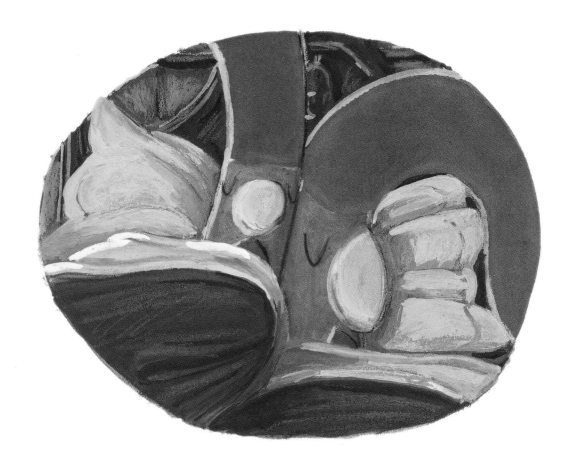

THE END

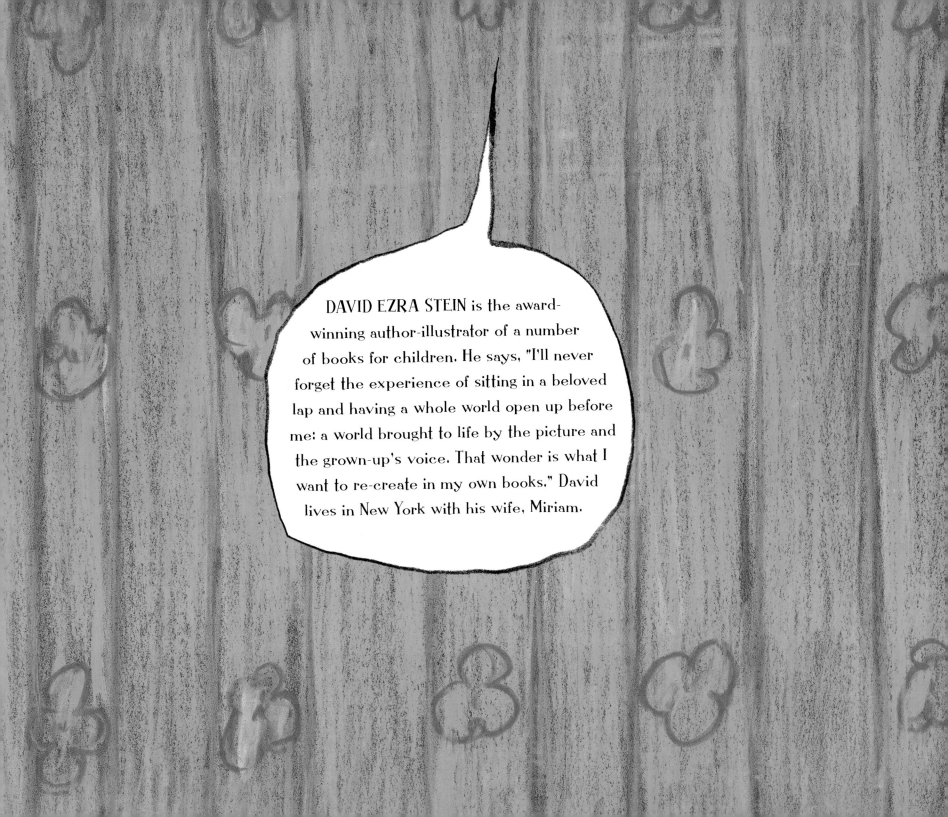

DAVID EZRA STEIN is the award-winning author-illustrator of a number of books for children. He says, "I'll never forget the experience of sitting in a beloved lap and having a whole world open up before me: a world brought to life by the picture and the grown-up's voice. That wonder is what I want to re-create in my own books." David lives in New York with his wife, Miriam.

For Bibi

Many thanks to Rebecca, Sarah and Ann for helping put this book to bed.

First published 2011 by Walker Books Ltd
87 Vauxhall Walk, London SE11 5HJ

This edition published 2012

2 4 6 8 10 9 7 5 3 1

© 2010 David Ezra Stein

The right of David Ezra Stein to be identified as author/illustrator
of this work has been asserted by him in accordance with
the Copyright, Designs and Patents Act 1988

This book has been typeset in Malonia Voigo

Printed in China

British Library Cataloguing in Publication Data:
a catalogue record for this book is available from the British Library

ISBN 978-1-4063-4031-0

www.walker.co.uk